SHADOW IN A JAR

I0585531

Short stories for shadow fiends

BOON

Pikey Camp

Shadow in a Jar
Copyright © 2018 by Boon.

For information contact :
pikeycamp@gmail.com
https://pikeycamp.wixsite.com/boon
Shadow in a Jar @pikeycamp

Book and Cover design by Boon
ISBN-13: 978-0-692-17358-9

First Edition: Month 2018

10 9 8 7 6 5 4 3 2 1

CONTENTS

The Mad Priest..1

Planet Atlantis..9

Old Man Reedus..19

Shadow in a Jar..29

Polyester Suits at the Pink Flamingo Inn........................53

The Golden Band..61

About the Author..67

Acknowledgements...68

THE MAD PRIEST

Deep in the swamps, there is an old haunted chapel. Creepy as a childhood nightmare, it is rumored to have been foolishly constructed upon an ancient sacred mound. Of course, the self righteous white settlers arrogantly built their place of worship at the top. It reminded them of the place where their saviour gave his life for their undeserving souls. But, there is no God here. No miracle man to forgive them of their unjust desecration or the innocent blood spilled as they stole this land in His name. Under the veil of ignorance, they didn't realize their murderous ways spawned a different kind of redemption. On this holy ground, rotted things came creeping back to life and purged the cancerous intruders back to the coast and away from the heart of the swamp. Although hundreds of years have passed, the old twisted and spindly chapel still stands on that sacred mound. Rumored tongues whisper horrifying stories of unfortunate investigators whose curiosity had gotten the better of them. Never to be seen or heard from again. These tales were only whispered and never spoken too loudly. For fear kept even the bravest of tongues from having these tales carried on the wind to fall on the ears of those rotted things, or even worse, the priest that yet still lives within the haunted chapel.

Under a gibbous moon, footsteps lightly thumped the river bank. Her path, somewhat fearless, direct to the haunted chapel. An undaunted determination fueled not by curiosity or foolish righteousness but of revenge. Fueled by hatred in its most maniacal form. Hatred for a priest from a witch of another sort. Not a wart-nosed witch or one of green skin that melts from water. A hybrid of sorts. Her bloodline ran deep into the past and in different directions. A voodoo queen conceived from an extraordinary twist of fate. Her blood of mixed descent. Irish, Haitian and Native American. Although knowledge of her voodoo royalty was a tight lipped kept secret, legend of her beauty had stretched out as far as words can travel. Most of all, her soul piercing eyes. Eyes of power. A fire-storm of wrath raged within her. She knew how to handle the rotted things that would stand between her and the haunted chapel, but confidence faltered beyond its doors. She understood the power within the chapel was beyond human comprehension. Yet, she was ultimately set on revenge. In her heart, she knew she was up against something much bigger than herself, way beyond her power. But, no turning back. She had committed herself to the task at hand and to the death of either her or the priest. With every step logic berated her. How foolish the idea. How ridiculous the notion.

But, revenge was her blindfold. She needed what lurked beyond those haunted doors. Nothing would stop her. Not venomous spiders nor poisonous water moccasins, not even behemoth alligators that lie in wait and hungry. Black panthers not even black bears or any other natural predator of the swamp would stand in her way. She left prepared. Razor sharp machete in hand to clear the path or to remove any limbs that reach for her. A magik'd up lamp to show her the way as well as to scurry off the lesser rotted things. Blood magiks and incantations done with entrails, grave dirt and sacrificial lamb would get her passed the others. As she splashed through the marsh, serpentine bodies slithered around her calves. The curiously warm water almost knee deep. Red eyes reflected the lantern light back at her, they were everywhere. Completely surrounded by creatures of the night and engulfed in the sound of the swamp, the midnight song of insects and wild critters. Her pace was strong and steady until something rotten gripped her right ankle. The abrupt halt threw her off balance, threatened to dowse her enchanted lamp.

"No!" Even though her teeth were clenched, the word escaped her beautiful mouth. The moonlight flashed on her razor sharp machete blade as it arced down, the rotted thing now less a limb. She managed to regain her stride, probably through sheer force of will. Hours of trudging through marsh, muck and swamp passed. She saw a certain silhouette against the star filled sky. The void shape of her destination. The haunted chapel that seemed only to exist in legend. Fierce determination carried her to the edge of the clearing. The ominous chapel majestically stood defiantly on top its earthen mound throne. It wasn't until then she noticed the thick humid air and the bullet sized beads of sweat that rolled down her porcelain smooth skin to further saturate sweat drenched clothes. For a brief moment, she stared at the marsh mud that caked up her boots and legs. Looking back up again, an enormous man shaped thing suddenly towered in front of her. In her peripheral, she noticed a horde of swamp things lumbering toward her from every direction. Her cold stare did not waver from the unnatural beast that stood before her. With pursed lips and clenched teeth she uttered,

"Get. Out. Of my way."

As unnatural of a creature it was, so was the bassy booming voice that came out of it somewhere,

"You are not welcome here. Only death awaits you."

"We'll see about that." With a sidestep and a mad dash up the mound, she was at the doors of the chapel. She cast a quick incantation and poured a line of salt with other unspeakable ingredients between her and the approaching rotted things. A magik barrier to keep them out and away from her objective, the mad priest. As the legend goes, the chapel is haunted by the ghost of a priest gone insane, but she knew the truth. Yes, it is true the priest is insane, but he is no ghost. He is a vampire. Once an innocent devout man of God caught in the middle of an unnatural war waged on the self righteous. Driven to madness with the realization he had become one of the eternally damned. A demon creature of hell, yet still devout and faithful to God. The vampire priest. Her confidence unwavering until she touched the cold slightly deteriorated door. No longer a resident of her chest, her heart now beat with the force of a sledge hammer at the back of her throat. Unable to swallow like the moment before vomiting, she pushed the door open and stepped in. Hundreds of prayer candles instantaneously lit by unseen hands and the door slammed shut behind her. The hair stood on the back of her neck. A faint smell of burning flesh mingled with a musty stench. Goose bumps textured her entire body when she noticed the enormous statue of Christ suspended from the chapel ceiling. Arms outstretched to receive his flock. Wrapped up like a mummy, but head exposed along with holed hands and holed feet. The suspended statue easily twenty-five feet in length. A few more cautious steps forward she heard sobbing, something reminiscent to human. She made out a word here and there. Maybe bits of a prayer intertwined with confessions of blasphemous acts of un-human violence. A few steps more and she saw him. The blood in her veins turned to ice water.

She was frozen. Body petrified. Fear all encompassing, all consuming. The source of burning flesh she had faintly caught a whiff of earlier now known to her. It was him. The mad priest. In the center of the chapel he was. Directly under the giant Christ. Cradling what was presumably the golden steeple that once adorned the top of this place of worship. Rocking back and forth, he desperately cradled the golden cross like a newborn infant. Oblivious to the searing of his undead flesh. Smoke rose from his body and swirled all the way up and around the enormous hovering Jesus.

Survival instincts screamed, "Run!" But, she could not. Although fright had control of her outer shell, it could not extinguish the inner flame of hatred that still burned inside. Revenge too hard a flame to snuff out. Her ice blood began to thaw. Her pounding heart slid back into its place, but continued its sledgehammer frenzy. She attempted to speak.

"I..."

Not even a blink of an eye and he was upon her. The tips of his clawed hand were on her throat, very nearly to the point of puncturing her skin. One ill move on her part and she would remove her own trachea. His smoldering flesh healed as he spoke.

"Why have you come here?" He asked with a whisper. She heard his voice more so in her mind than from his lips. She dropped machete and lamp from her hands. Before they hit the ground he was hanging from giant Christ.

"Ssspeak, witch." His whisper echoed from

everywhere.

She had never witnessed power such as this. Indescribable terror she felt at that moment. Trembling, she tried to form words.

"I... I..." was all she managed to get out.

And he was upon her again except this time he held her in the air by her throat. Her feet dangled far from the floor.

"Ssspeak witch or be forever sssilencced." His fingers began constricting air from throat. She knew she was moments from death, even worse, failure.

"He raped my little boy!" Clawed fingers loosened grip to allow her to speak a bit easier. "He raped my little boy and... drowned him in the baptism pool."

The vampire priest gently lowered her to the floor.

"Who did thisss?"

"Father Adams," she whimpered, but hate cut through. "And others from the church. They're raping and murdering our children."

A single tear of blood ran down undead cheek.

"How do you know thisss?"

"Seance... I spoke with the dead. My little boy hadn't come home. I knew something was wrong. I summoned the dead... and my precious little boy came to me." She broke. Crying the most heart broken cry humanly possible. The vampire priest held her close to where his heart once beat and lovingly stroked her hair.

She regained composure.

"I didn't realize until then... so many children had gone missing lately. They were all there... with my little boy.

It was Father Adams... and his people."

"Sssurely you have the power to deal with thessse murderersss."

"I do. But... I want... I need more than death for them."

"I sssee. Sssuch comesss with a priccce."

"Of course. And I'll gladly pay."

The vampire priest looked into her beautiful eyes now swollen from tears.

"You will harvessst sssoulsss for me. Harvessst sssoulsss of evil men."

"I will do this for you," she said.

"And I will bring more than death to thossse who murdered the children. Even more ssso for the one who murdered your ssson."

PLANET ATLANTIS

1936 Cairo.

Mystery begets curiosity. I'm an adventurer. I have
experienced strange narratives and weird events that
defy all believability. I have documented my travels,
discoveries and epiphanies. Now, dark miasmal
depression is all-consuming, all encompassing my
apocalyptic realization. For this will certainly be my last
entry. Hundreds, perhaps thousands of years from
now, an adventurer obsessed such as I will one day
discover this diary, my dusty bones and ugly skull. My
unfortuitous predicament is the result of my recent
obsession with Egyptology and ancient Sumer.
Upon arrival of ancient and mysterious Cairo, I
discovered myself in awe of this place I had only

explored in books and daydreams. Antiquity is still very much alive in this exotic part of the world. Labyrinths of brick alleyways, cobbled streets and market squares full of undulating traffic. Foreign languages spoken by native tongue yelling, conversing and bartering. Laughter, crying, the moans of the blind, beggars and cripples. The sounds of money exchanging hands, beasts of burden pulling carts. Camels and donkeys snorting and braying. A full spectrum of turbans, veils, beads and silk. A barrage of countless aromas, incense, perfume and food cooking. All under a stubborn sky of endless blue.

It is paramount that I remain incognito. Germans are in charge of all excavations. Their knowledge of my presence must be avoided at all costs. Loose tongues paid well tell of their search for ancient antediluvian relics of esoteric nature. Their fuhrer, consumed with obsession, just as I it seems. Which lends strength to my speculation. My obsession. Mysterious Egypt. No other place has intrigued me so. It's megalithic cyclopean structures, monolithic obelisks and statues carved from diorite and red granite. All to a level of perfection that we cannot reproduce with modern technology. It boggles the mind as to why they chose to build in the most difficult and impossible way. But, I cannot afford to ramble on. My last candle is waxing, the light waning. It won't be long until I am in total darkness.

At sunrise, I met with my guide, Aziz, an energetic youth with an honest demeanor and firm grasp of the English language. Although unlicensed, he is highly recommended by my peers of exceptional credulity. We set out with a packed camel for the fabled forgotten sphinx. A second sphinx that has been lost in antiquity. For it is my speculation that we are a species with amnesia and have forgotten a critical part of our story. Deduction resulting from extensive scientific and historical research led Aziz and I on a full day's journey to a ragged opening in the ground. Before the vertiginous descent by rope into the narrow hewn well, I looked upon the ominous sands of the desert rolling and incoherently whispering nefarious ancient secrets. The red sun sank into the eternal shimmering desert followed by the relentless chill of desert night. It would be my last experience above the ground.

The twenty-foot rope descent down the irregular hewn stone well was rough going and physically demanding. At the bottom, the moon pierced darkness into large shards of occulant void. I searched the underground chambers for two days, Aziz just as excited and fascinated by the romance of pre-history. I discovered subterranean passages beneath the lost Sphinx leading to depths none may dare to imagine. Depths connected with mystery older than dynastic Egypt, possibly even Sumer. I discovered a perfectly square shaft inexplicably carved from diorite. Only just large enough for me to crawl uncomfortably. Exploration demanded I enter. Aziz, being smaller than I, suggested he lead with the lantern. I agreed with his reasoning, but with great reluctance. I endured thirty feet of the claustrophobic torturing space, then the suffocating crawl dropped to a sudden hellish angle. The horror of the experience deepened with a very perceptible increase in the rate of my descent. I scraped brutally against the sides of the stone shaft. Nails ripped from my fingers with every futile attempt to slow the almost straight shot down. The speed and incredible depth of it robbed me of my cognitive faculties. Sliding furiously into the unholy fathomless dark of nether Earth. The shocking ordeal was cumulative. Culminating to grotesque. Consciousness teetered back and forth on the slippery edge of twilight. Judging by the amount of stubble on my face, I must have been out for at least a day or two. My nostrils were assailed by a creeping odor of damp and staleness with overtones of incense and spices. The battery-powered lamp lying next to Aziz was miraculously intact and functioning, but it's battery low. The light only a dim glow barely keeping pitch darkness at bay. My initial steady stream of consciousness afflicted by confusion and lapse of memory. Then the mental cataclysm came. It was horrible and hideous beyond all articulate description. The fall broke my lower right leg in at least nine places and felt more akin to a sock full of marbles. Blood had trickled from everywhere. I called out to Aziz, there was no answer. Agonizing pain induced nausea from flipping myself over. I drug myself with bloody hands to him. Aziz was lying on his belly, but his head was turned around beyond human capacity and facing me. Eyes wide open, dull and lifeless. The weight of

sadness I felt was profound and remorseful.
I cobbled together a splint from expired torches and
the cloth windings that once adorned Aziz's head. I
discovered myself to be in a massive hall of knowledge.
I was forced to silence by sheer awe. Countless shelves
and cubbyholes with columns of papyrus scrolls,
tablets made of clay, stone, emerald, copper and other
various biblioteki. There must be four hundred
thousand to seven hundred thousand texts. I was able
to translate an engraving high above on the wall. "The
place of the cure of the soul". This must have been a
library of sorts or a research center or perhaps an
antediluvian university. I skimmed over several texts.
The knowledge contained here can advance the modern
world at least a thousand years or more. It is beyond
the scope of reasoning the extent these ancient people
went to gather historical and cultural documentation
from all over the world of scientific research, including
physics, astronomy and medicine. I can only imagine
the pure ecstasy the likes of Hipparchus, Euclid,
Dionysus Thrax or Herophilus or Archimedes,
Eratosthenes, or Heron of Alexandria would experience
in this great hall. The prospect of such antiquity and
knowledge contained within filled me with great
reverence and immensity. The answer to all of history's
mysteries and the irony is overwhelming. Limited to
only a few hours of light. Aziz's lamp faded to
uselessness. Only a handful of candles remained.
I made a Herculean attempt at conserving light. Fever
from internal infection set in. Panic insued. There is no

way out. No doors or corridors. The shaft from which Aziz and I fell to our doom is beyond even the failing light's reach. It must have been a fourteen foot drop. I will translate what I can before the darkness overtakes me. I scoured dozens of texts written in Sumerian cuneiform. Lamentation texts found bewailing the destruction and desolation of varying Sumerian cities. All of these texts blame the destruction on the use of a weapon of terror and a deadly cloud.

After a few days of finishing the last rations, the despicable notion of cannibalism entered my dazed but mostly coherent mind. Even if I could bring myself to commit such a heinous blasphemy, there is not enough burning material to cook poor Aziz. Only the ancient scrolls remain which are more important than my own life. It leaves one diabolical resort. I would be forced to eat Aziz raw. I cannot bring myself to that level of self-preservation. I cannot eat Aziz nor burn the ancient texts. I will forfeit. I would consume my own flesh, but I am not that survivor type. I will continue to translate these ancient texts until the light is no more.

What I discovered next can only be compared to touching the face of God. I have solved the mystery of Atlantis. Emerald green tablets engraved with cuneiform script document a bizarre and intriguing story. This is my crowning achievement, I discovered the mythical lost city in an ancient hall of records buried beneath the sands, soon to be my tomb. A highly advanced civilization wiped from the face of the planet, only to leave behind megalithic clues to its existence.

The myth now congruent with logic. As my last candle flickers, I make my last entry. My greatest discovery.

"They created their own planet. The vision of a prodigy geoengineer known as Aeonoas. An unavoidable catastrophic event threatened mass extinction to his home world. Although regarded as the greatest visionary of their people, Aeonoas suffered harsh and resounding ridicule after announcing his plan for survival. His vision of a breakaway civilization. He designed a space vessel the size of a small moon and named it Wyrmwood. Basalt dust collected from an asteroid belt and a layer of mica covered Wyrmwood's outer titanium shell. Volcanic rock and metal dust measuring a few miles thick insulated the twenty mile thick shell making it virtually impervious to the cosmic menaces of deep space. Aeonoas amassed genetic code of every life form that existed on the doomed planet along with all recorded knowledge of his people. The all encompassing construct of his planet's ecosystem harboured in space ark Wyrmwood. Aeonoas with a crew of eight hundred embarked on a million year trek to the closest planet most similar to their own ill fated home world. From solar system to solar system the rogue moon journeyed through space fixed on the fastest route to its destination. One of the most god like feats ever achieved in all of history. Aeonoas and crew woke from the deep sleep as Wyrmwood entered a young solar system. As the intergalactic refugees approached their new planet, Aeonoas calculated various celestial positions for Wyrmwood to reside. He decided on one that Wyrmwood and the new mother planet would enjoy a mathematical relationship, a

fixed rotation and synchronous orbit turning on a common center. He even calculated a beautiful cosmic dance of sun moon scissoring. Wyrmwood was also designed to be a counterbalance. Only a stabilized planet with tides and seasons could sustain the diverse and complex ecosystem preserved in the space ark. Aeonoas planned Wyrmwood to strengthen the new mother planet's magnetosphere, as well. His artistic genius became fully realized as he calculated Wyrmwood to perfectly cover the face of the young solar system's star, only the star's corona to be seen during an eclipse. Aeonoas wanted the occasional eclipse to be beautiful and perfect, to be the pupil of the All Creator.

New Mother World experienced several cataclysmic events as Wyrmwood positioned itself in the heavens. Global flooding, earthquakes and volcanic eruptions combined with planetary electric discharges annihilated most of New World's terrestial species into extinction. Aeonoas and crew waited with patience as New Mother Planet stabilized with a more suitable atmosphere.

Aeonoas and crew descended to the terra farmed world. They named it Atlantis and proclaimed themselves to be gods, nothing they could not achieve. Populated it with life from Old Planet. The New Gods established a global civilization. They constructed megalithic structures to harness the planet's energy. A technology based on harmonizing geological resonance. A symbiotic existence thrived.

Some New Gods were genetically curious. Controversial experiments produced genetic engineered hybrids and fierce arguments concerning moral ethics. No combination remained unadulterated. Using New God genetic code and

*the DNA of New Mother Planet, they fashioned a being in
their own image and named this hybrid species Adamu.
New Gods cherished Adamu, allowed them to procreate and
multiply. Some New Gods took Adamu as wives, an act
considered taboo and frowned upon. Procreation between
New Gods and Adamu caused much strife. The first crack in
their society. The crack spider webbed.
Once a harmonious utopia, Atlantis became adulterated
with violence. New Gods went to war with giants, other
extra terrestial gods and most grievous their precious
Adamu. Atlantis in turmoil did not expect what was coming.
During Wyrmwood's million year trek, it attracted a planet
destroying comet which trailed far behind. The comet
followed Wyrmwood and planetary calamity followed the
New Gods. Abandon Atlantis, The New Gods decided.
Adamu did not have time to prepare for the cataclysm. The
comet smashed into the planet. A global deluge rendered
almost all life extinct."*

Wyrmwood, what we know to be our moon, stabilized
the distressed planet yet again. A small number of
Adamu survived, but were scattered over the planet.
They did their best to retain as much knowledge of
their world, but lost most. Even that precious
knowledge was fractured and puzzling. As time
moved on, they forgot who they were and how they
came to be, but the ever resilient Adamu multiplied.
Civilization had a new identity, but one with amnesia.
It moved forward and renamed its mother world,
Earth.

My faculties are convoluted and sluggish from internal infection caused by broken bones, dehydration and starvation. Even in this feverish state, I still cannot eat Aziz. Unavoidably, the fever will soon boil my brains to expiration. I will forfeit. Lay my bones down in the darkness and wait for death.

OLD MAN REEDUS

"Here he is!" Dirk exclaimed, catching hold of the naked vagrant by the arm.

"Wha... what?" the filth sodden face replied. He was sizing up the group of men who suddenly had him at bay. Four of them. Under the bridge they'd found him sleeping. Far enough away from town that no cry for help would reach any human ears. "What do you want with me?"

"You've been seen walking around naked. Exposing yourself to the good people of this town without any disregard," Dirk said.

The filthy man winced. Drivel oozed from the corner of his mouth and a fine mist of saliva spewed into the air, "The hell you say!"

Gilbo ambled up to the old man, "What's your

name?" he queried with ambiguous tone. Much taller
and robust than Dirk, his scabrous demeanor left no
question that Gilbo was well acquainted with violence.
Edging even closer, "What's. Your. Name?" His eyes
flickered with vicious intent.

"Reedus," the old man reluctantly answered.

Gilbo's craggy face split sideways with a grin that
revealed a few broken teeth. "Well then. Mr. Reedus."
Beads of sweat began rolling down the old man's face
taking with it a layer of dirt leaving behind several
trails of pasty white skin. A drippy painting come to
life. The alcohol on his breath was a strong kick to the
face, but his body odor much more repugnant.

"For fuck sake, I can smell his balls from here,"
Christo said. Noticing a swarm of tiny gnats buzzing
around the old man's head and genitals, "Where's your
clothes then, eh?"

Gilbo pushed Reedus back hard enough to make his
teeth click. The old man lost his footing and tumbled
over the make shift shelter he had cobbled together
from debris and whatever else he pulled out of the
river. Bottles clanked together. A familiar sound to
those who frequent the pub.

"Ooh... You heard that gents? He's got some goods
in there, doesn't he?" Gilbo exclaimed with delight.
"Satch, see what you can find in that heap of rubbish."
"Right," Satch replied. Before he could get to pilfering
Reedus was surprisingly back on his feet to protect his
belongings.

"No! It's mine!" Reedus cried and pushed Satch

away.

"Oooooooo," the quartet said in chorus.

"We know you got balls, old man. We can smell them. But I didn't think they were made of brass," Glibo chuckled. With that said, Gilbo planted his fist in the middle of Reedus's muck gilded face.

Lightning struck every nerve ending in the old man's body and blood began to pour from the long hair of his nostrils. He was momentarily blinded by his watering eyes. The thought of these ruffians thieving his booze enraged him. He swung his fists wildly and blindly.

"Oh dear, this is about to get messy," said Christo and looked away. Christo didn't have the stomach for what usually comes next. One too many times Christo saw the flash of a straight razor followed by loops of guts spilling onto the ground.

Dirk and Gilbo each caught hold of an arm restraining Reedus.

"You've got some fight in you yet, you old codger!" Dirk guffawed. "But, you're going to want to settle down before you end up on the wrong side of a sharp blade."

The threat didn't seem to register. Reedus was locked on Satch tearing apart the crude shelter.

"Aaaahh, a few bottles of hooch... a book... and a bunch of rubbish."

"Are there any trousers?" asked Christo. "Can we at least get his dick covered with something?"

"No. No clothes. You've got booze but no clothes, old

man?" Satch erupted with laughter.

Speaking the tongue of inebriation Reedus slurred a soft spoken threat, "I'll kill you. I'll kill you all."

"What's that?" Gilbo asked. "Say that again. Say it. One. More. Time."

The old man turned his dirty now bloodied face to Gilbo with a smile so beautiful and perfect that it gutted Gilbo somewhere inside. Although the alcohol made his words heavy and encumbering to speak, Reedus echoed, "I. Will. Kill. You."

Gilbo was triggered. A barrage of blows unleashed upon the old man and his body fell limp within moments. As anyone unfortunate enough to be on the receiving end of an attack such as this and lived, they would surely testify that Gilbo's fists were hard as concrete. That's if they still retained the memory and ability to speak.

Dirk and Christo managed to pull Gilbo off the old man.

Christo shouted, "That's enough! That's enough!"

Gilbo in frenzy mode connected a concrete block fist with the unsuspecting forehead of Christo. The blow sent Christo reeling backwards and horizontal onto the ground.

"What the hell, Gilbo! Calm the fuck down!" Dirk cried.

Sentience revealed itself to Gilbo. He stood over the old man's body, fists dripping warm thick blood. "Kill me? Mr. Reedus?! Really?!" With dark red splattered face Gilbo spat upon the slack body. He then walked down to the river and splashed the blood from his face and washed his hands. "Give me a bottle of that hooch."

A couple hours had passed. They used what was left of the old man's shelter to build a fire. With each at the bottom of a bottle of booze, they were all speaking the tongue of inebriation. All except Christo. Drunk, yes. But not engaged in conversation with the others. He had been reading the book that Satch found. Except it really wasn't a book. It was a journal. Hand written presumably by Reedus. Christo would look up from time to time and stare at the old man's limp body in bewilderment. These were the best stories he had ever read in his life. Some were on the edge of intangible like a dream. Others were vivid in detail. Most were violent horrors that far exceeded any Gilbo rampage.

"Christo... Christo!" said Dirk.

"Huh? Wha...?" Christo didn't notice they were even there. Wondered if they had been talking to him all this time.

"What you got there?" asked Dirk.

"Nothing really. Just a silly book," Christo brushed off.

Gilbo erupted with laughter, "Well you look pretty fucking silly with my fist print still on your forehead!"

Satch cracked in a fit of laughter so hard he nearly pissed himself.

"You know... You can be a real asshole, Gilbo," Christo said.

23

"Yeah I know. Mr. Reedus found that out the hard way," Gilbo answered with a broke tooth grin.

"Well, I'm off. It's a long walk back." Christo was on his feet and on his way to a derelict shack just on the edge of town. Although it leaked like a sieve, it kept most of the elements out. He was almost sober by the time he made it there. As usual, he didn't bother changing into sleeping attire. The cot creaked and moaned with the weight of his body. He couldn't stop thinking about Mr. Reedus. How did the old man end up living under a bridge? Surely a talent such as his would have been recognized. Maybe he was famous at one point in his life. Lost his fame and fortune and then became a drunken hobo? Christo pulled the book from his pocket and began reading once again. His eyelids were heavy, but the bottom of each page coerced him to continue reading. The twilight of sleep eventually overpowered his will for consciousness. The next morning, Christo woke with an impending resolve. He decided to go back to the bridge and bury old man Reedus. A talent such as his deserved at least that much. With shovel in hand, Christo set out to do what was the most honorable act he had ever done. Christo surprised himself at the thought of it. The walk out of town to the bridge didn't seem to take as long this time around. As he approached the foot of the bridge, Christo scanned the road for travellers. After confirmation of no one in the vicinity, he took the worn path that lead under the bridge. He noticed the smell of burnt wood, the remains of the campfire was still smoldering as he approached.

"What in the actual hell happened here?" escaped on impulse. This was not the scene Christo left the night before. Dark red soaked the river bank with large ominous puddles. Did Gilbo gut the old man open to watch the blood run out? But the amount of blood here would fill more than one Mr. Reedus. Did Gilbo finally breach sanity into the insane, mutilating his friends? Christo's mind was flooded with scenarios trying to rationalize. This state of shock and bewilderment dulled his awareness. He did not notice Mr. Reedus emerging from the river behind.

"Looking for your friends?" a now completely sober and clean Mr. Reedus said.

"Oh shit!" Christo spun around with a jump. "I thought Gilbo killed you. I thought you were dead."

"So did they. What's with the shovel?" Reedus asked.

"I... I was going to give you a proper burial."

"Proper burial," replied Reedus, more of statement than question.

"Well... yes. We found your book. I... I read your stories. You're a brilliant writer, Mr. Reedus. I felt you deserved to be buried. Not picked apart by animals," Christo spouted. "You did write them, didn't you?"

"Ah, my journal... those aren't stories. They're memories."

"Memories?" Christo said in utter confusion.

"Yes," Reedus smiled a perfect beautiful smile. Something about the look in the old man's eye was disturbing. A sudden chill washed over Christo. His grip white knuckled the shovel handle as his heart elevated and began to pound. "What happened to them?" Christo demanded frantically. Rationale was still accessible, a scene began to play out in Christo's mind. Dirk, Satch and Gilbo passed out around the campfire? The old man must have regained consciousness, found Gilbo's blade and slit their throats? That would explain the excessive amount of blood on the river bank. "What did you do to them?! Where's Dirk and Satch?"

"You're forgetting Gilbo," the old man's smile widened a bit more. He took a step towards Christo.

"Don't come any closer, old man!"

"I meant what I said," the old man's smile widened even further showing an impossible number of teeth. The entirety of his eyes suddenly went black. "I'll kill you all." The old man's fingernails grew into talons. His jaw unhinged itself to reveal multiple rows of jagged teeth.

Christo had only a mere moment to rationalize the transformation of the old man before him. It didn't matter, nor did raising the shovel in defense. Old man Reedus was upon him. Razor sharp talons sliced through flesh and bone. The shovel dropped to the ground with white knuckles and forearms still attached. Blood spewed. Christo had let out a short lived muffled scream of terror. The unhinged jaw and rows of teeth removed Christo's head at the neck with one bite. Its often said that one's life flashes before one's eyes at the moment of death. Not so for Christo.

The last thing his bodiless head witnessed was the belly of old man Reedus.

Shadow in a Jar

Ominous clouds lumbered. The sky degenerated from blue to charcoal grey. The smell of rain and ozone rode in on the back of a breeze. When a flash of lightning lit up the foreboding sky, she decided to make her way back to town. Breeze became wind. Lightning spider webbed itself around the belly of the sky. Another connected sky to ground. Outrunning the storm was an unrealistic expectation, confirmed when the bottom of the sky gave way to a torrential downpour. She needed shelter.

Vesper took refuge in a dilapidated shack on the outskirts of town. She had no idea whom it belonged to, but it was obvious the shack had been abandoned for some time. Fetid dankness filled her nose with the shack's decaying interior. It leaked like a seive. The roof bowed and barely held itself together. Rainwater cascaded down from several places like little waterfalls collecting in puddles.

She moved a decrepit looking table and matching chair to the most non-leakiest part of the room. On the table, a worn out journal called her attention. She opened the book, but the storm obscured the sun and there wasn't enough light to read. She pilfered around the old shack until an old beat up oil lamp presented itself. Vesper placed the lamp on the table. The cracked glass dome missed a few pieces within it's metal cage. Her reflection mimicked her motions as she struck a few failed matches.

"How do I end up in situations like this," she sighed a deep sigh of self-pity. She paused for a moment of contemplation and gazed at her reflection. The last match sizzled into flame producing a crooked smile on her cute face. The acrid smell of sulphur broke the shack of it's rot bouquet for a few moments. She wasn't going anywhere soon, so she began to explore the old pages. The flickering light and thunderstorm lent itself well to the creepy stories handwritten in the old worn book.

After reading a few pages, the storm reduced to a backdrop for the stage play in her mind. She read almost the entire book before sleep overtook her. Vesper woke to the sound of a music box song. With book in hand, she stepped out of the dilapidated shack and into a beautiful morning. All the tree tops leaned slightly in the same direction. Fallen branches and leaves decorated the landscape. Somehow, the world seemed clean again and smelled new. The music grew louder. In the distance she saw a horse and wagon on the road heading into town. The music box song emanated from the wagon.

Vesper stood at the side of the road amazed by the sight. The wagon was not a wagon at all. It was a cottage on wagon wheels. A quaint little cottage complete with chimney, slate roof, gas lights, sash windows and planter boxes full of various plants and ivy. The horse wasn't a horse either. It was an automaton full of steam, gears and brass engineered to the anatomically correct likeness of a champion-blooded Clydesdale. It was the most stunning steam machine she had ever seen. A mechanized masterpiece of brilliance, ingenuity and gilded brass. Steam exhausted from the mechanical horse nostrils. It startled Vesper out of her trance. As the wagon slowed and stopped, so did the music. A middle aged man stood behind the steering wheel. He was a distinguished gentlemen of charming demeanor.

"As you stand there in amazement by my wondrous equine automaton, allow me to introduce myself. I'm the incredible Silas Newton, master of shadows!" said the driver, removing his top hat extending into a deep bow.

"Oh wow," she said barely over a whisper. The mysterious stranger spoke with an elegant accent she heard only once before as a child. Her cheeks flushed. Taken by fantastical charm of the experience she gave

an awkward curtsy and replied, "I'm Vesper."
"Pleased to meet you, miss Vesper. Might I trouble you
to point me in the direction to the telegram facility?"
asked Silas.
Vesper giggled, "Sure, for a ride to town. I'll direct you
to the 'telegram facility'." She emphasized 'telegram
facility' imitating Silas's accent.
Vesper climbed into the seat next to Silas. He pulled
a few levers and released the brake. Steam billowed
out of mechanized horse nostrils. The music began
to play as the wagon began moving. Possessed by
uncontrollable giddiness Vesper gave in to a fit of
laughter.
"So, what brings you to Tiger Island, incredible-Silas-
Newton-master-of-shadows?" Vesper smiled. It was
Silas's turn to fall prey to her charm.
"I'm an entertainer. Shadow puppets. I'm performing
tonight at the Sea Wall Theater."
"Oh yeah, now I get it. I haven't seen a shadow show
since I was a little girl. Where did you get the steam
horse? It's magnificent."
"I built it. With the help of a few friends. The caravan
as well."
"The music box song is a nice touch. I haven't seen
anything like it."
"Yes, it attracts attention from the most curious of
creatures indeed."

A twenty foot tall brick wall encompassed the town of

Tiger Island. Brass and copper pipes of various sizes ranging from tiny to enormous lined the inner wall and connected to steam powered water pumps the size of circus elephants. Engineered for protection from flood waters which rose annually. Not long after passing the wall, the song of the giant music box attracted much attention. The crowd grew larger cheering and applauding the mechanical horse and giant music box. "That's the telegram station, right over there." Vesper pointed to a small building across the street. "Thanks for the ride, Mr. Silas."

"You're very welcome, miss Vesper. Please, come to the show tonight, I'll put you on the guest list," said Silas.

"Sure, I'll be there," said Vesper." She jumped from the wagon and vanished into the mass of townsfolk.

Silas noticed an old worn book in the very same spot Vesper had just been.

"She forgot her book," Silas thought. Just as he was about to call out to her, a booming voice cracked like thunder and nearly startled him.

"I heard the song of a music box so enticingly hypnotic, I had to follow it! The song led me here to this masterful work of mechanical ingenuity. I must say, sir, I have a vast collection of steam automatons and machines, but none the likes of this. Please indulge as to where you acquired such a divine machine."

Hieronymus Pitt stood there bolstering a good six-foot and four inches. Dressed in pristine white from wide brim hat to calf high boots. A local celebrity famous for being the most powerful and wealthy.

"Greetings, kind sir." Silas pulled a few levers, engaged the brake and stepped down from the wagon. "I'm Silas Newton, entertainer and tinkerer. I did not acquire this bucket of bolts and gears, I built it myself with a little help from my friends. It's the only one of its kind."

"Marvelous, absolutely marvelous. Your foreign articulation tells me that you are a long way from home."

"Indeed," said Silas, extending his hand.

"I'm Hieronymus Pitt. On behalf of Tiger Island, I welcome you to our humble town. Forgive me, I don't shake hands."

"No offense taken. And I thank the good folk of Tiger Island for having me. I'll be performing at the Sea Wall Theater and I would be delighted to have you as my guest."

"Why thank you, sir. I am very familiar with the Sea Wall Theater. I own it. You'll find that I own just about everything around here," he said with a smile and wink. "And if I don't own it now," Hieronymus paused to admire the brass and iron Clydesdale, "I soon will."

Something flashed in Hieronymus's eyes for a split moment. Although barely imperceptible, it managed to arch Silas's left brow.

Silas walked into the small building that served as Sheriff's office, telegram services and courier delivery. Two jail cells to his left, a large wooden desk to his right. Behind the desk sat a scrawny pale officer. With a large smile, he greeted Silas.

"How can I help you there, fella? What can we do you

for?"

"Good afternoon, kind sir," Silas tilted his top hat with a nod.

The officer chuckled, "We don't get many foreigners around here. Where you from?" asked officer.

"The old world," Silas said, scanning the room.

For a moment, Silas's attention focused on the one occupied cell. Inside it, a young man of athletic build shadowboxed in the corner. Silas's left eyebrow arched, mouth pursed to one side. His attention turned back to the officer.

"Allow me to introduce myself, I'm Silas Newton. I'm performing tonight at the Sea Wall Theater."

"Oh, I should have figured as much. You're the shadow puppet fella everyone been a hooting and hollering about," officer said. "Pleased to meet you, I'm officer Roper."

"Indeed," Silas smoothed his gray and black peppered beard to a point. "Officer Roper, I need to send a telegram."

"Oh sure, sure. I can do that for you no problem," Roper said. He went into the drawer, out with a paper and ready for dictation.

"Arrived at Tiger Island noon stop. S stop N stop." said Silas.

"Is that all?" Roper asked.

"Yes, sir." Silas reached into his vest pocket and presented a card to the officer. "To this address. And, I'll be needing to send another telegram later tonight, immediately after the show."

"Oh sure, sure. That's no problem. I won't be here, but Vin will be. He'll take care of you, no problem."

"I've noticed you have incarcerated one of The Fancy." Silas said, turning to observe the shadow boxer.

"Ah hell, yessir! That there is Jacky Hammer," Roper said, almost as if he didn't believe his own words.

"The gypsy boxer?" asked Silas with furled brow.

"Yes, sir. Jacky the sledge Hammer," said Roper. "Say, Jacky!" Roper called out to the shadow boxer. "Tell this fine gentleman who you are."

The shadow boxer turned around, gracefully throwing punches and kicking up dust from the floor with fancy footwork.

"I'm Jacky Hammer," His voice sounded like it rose from gravel. Coarse as a ferrier's rasp and wounded to the soul.

"You're one of The Fancy," Silas said as he approached the cell.

"Yeah, that's right. Brethren of the Gypsy Boxing Ring," Jacky said. Two noticeably oversized hands gripped the iron bars framing Jacky's baby face which, oddly enough, also possessed the giggle mug, a face in perpetual smile.

"Please to meet you Mr. Hammer. I'm Silas Newton, entertainer," Silas said removing his top hat with a bow. What a curious combination of genetics Silas pondered Jacky to be. "Time is always ticking. Tick, tock. I must prepare for tonight's events. I bid you fine gentlemen good day."

The sun retired into the horizon as night followed
to blanket the world. An undulant crowd stood on
cobbled street in front of the only theater in town.
Cigar and pipe smoke, laughter and chatter filled the
headroom. Inside, the Sea Wall Theater full of anxious
patrons. A singing guitar player known as Blind Boy
Rags opened the show. He wore a ragged top hat, a
dingy bandanna blindfolded his eyes and he played an
old beat up box guitar. His guitar playing lacked skill
but his voice dared a religious experience otherworldly
and captivating. The stage curtains closed at the end
of his set. In the lobby, tongues traded rumors of how
Rags sold his soul for a golden voice. The next day he
woke with an extraordinary singing voice, but during
the night as he slept, a demon took his eyes.
The stage curtains drew back as the house lights
dimmed. On each side of the stage stood a stack of
huge gramophone horns attached to a large music
box. It's metal tumbler exposed for all to see it's spiny
pattern pluck metal fingers. Silas walked onto the stage
to wind up the music box. He paused for a moment
scanning the audience. It was a full house. In the rows
of people, Vesper's cute face and unmistakable crooked
smile caught his attention. He tipped his top hat at her.
In his peripheral, Silas noticed Hieronymus staring
at Vesper, his face split wide with a smile ear to ear.
The crowd hushed itself to silence as the music began.
Silas stood behind a white flat curtain made of silk. It
stretched out to either side of the stage. He grabbed a
handful each of long finely crafted sticks. At the end of

the sticks, intricately ornate puppets made of rabbit and donkey skin. A light to cast shadow of puppets upon silk made the stage for stories that flowed through his skilled fingers. The entire theater fell entranced to the silhouettes and story. Charmed by the music box song. Silas told the story of an emperor from ancient times, madly in love with a beautiful concubine. She died the day before their wedding and he was heartbroken. As the wise advisor pondered the best ways to lift the emperor's spirits, he noticed shadows being cast through a parasol and inspiration illuminated an idea. That evening, the wise advisor prepared a screen and a light as well as the silhouette of a woman cut from leather. He told the Emperor to meet him at the courtyard at sundown. The wise advisor put on the first show of it's kind. The birth of shadow puppet theater. The emperor and his court were amazed. The shadow puppet reminded the emperor of his lost love. It brought him to tears. Later that night when the emperor was fast asleep, his lost love appeared to him in a dream. She floated in from the window and told him to stop mourning her and run the country well. Upon waking, the dream challenged reality. The emperor was revitalized after seeing his love and went on to rule the longest most prosperous times in his land's history.

Silas's show lasted about an hour. After the performance, Silas took several bows as the audience applauded. He looked for Vesper in the rows, but discovered her seat vacant. A darting glance found

Hieronymus's seat abandoned, as well.

This is baby sitting. Officer Vin thought this job would be an action packed adventure. Not in a small town like Tiger Island. Quite the opposite. Vin's days and nights blurred together into a repetitive montage. A ritual of life mundane blessed by boredom. Tonight marked his third week of working the graveyard shift. It seemed to him that even time was just going through the motions.

The door flew open so suddenly it startled officer Vin to his feet. In walked Silas Newton.

"Howdy, fella," officer Vin said. His pulse quickened and he felt a bit nervous. This was out of the ordinary. He wasn't familiar with out of the ordinary.

Silas glanced over his shoulder, Jacky Hammer sat up in his bunk. Shadows of iron cell bars across his face shifted with the flickering flame of gas lights.

"Kind sir, I need to send a telegram," said Silas.

"Hmmm. Alrighty," officer Vin relaxed, but his words were loaded with disappointment. He unconsciously sighed, licked his fingertips for better grip on the dictation paper. His eyes rolled as he prepared to take Silas's message.

"Show was a success stop. Leaving Tiger Island at the witching hour stop. S stop N stop." Silas pulled a card from his vest pocket and handed it to officer Vin, "to this address."

Officer Vin took the card and dictation to the telegram machine. "You must be that shadow puppet fella."
"Right you are, sir."
"I haven't seen a good show in a long time. Matter of fact, I haven't seen much of anything lately." Vin said.
"Well, my good man, allow me to remedy that." Silas reached into his pocket, but this time pulled out a small windup music box. He wound it up placed it on the desk next to the lantern.
The music box played its song. Vin sat back. His chair moaned from the shift in weight. Silas placed his hands in front of the lantern using it's light to project shadows on the wall.
The combination of music box song, flickering lantern and manipulated shadows on the wall were intoxicating. The shadows made from Silas's contorted hands defied logic. Jacky stood with his face pressed between the bars of his cell. The creepy music box song made the shadows creepier. Vin stood from his desk, took a few steps passed Silas. The shadow master contorted his hands in such a way it projected the silhouette of a skull. Vin stood there mesmerized by the skull shadow. His own shadow now cast on the wall in warped silhouette. The skull shadow opened its massive mouth and consumed Vin's shadow. Hair stood on Jacky's arms and neck. The sight beyond insanity. Vin's shadow no longer on the wall, but kicking and flailing to free itself from the grip of Silas Newton. Jacky shook his head from Vin to Silas stuffing a Vin-shaped shadow into a small glass jar,

then sealed with a cork. Vin didn't move. No more than a catatonic statue made of flesh and bone. Not even his clothes rustled.

"What the hell? You're in league with demons," Jacky said.

"No, I'm a demon hunter. Which is the exact opposite." Silas took the large skeleton key hanging on Vin's hip.

"But you just stole that man's shadow." Jacky couldn't quite get his mind around it.

"No," Silas said placidly. "It's only mine until daybreak." Silas returned the music box to his pocket. Using the key lifted from Vin, Silas unlocked and opened the cell door.

Jacky stepped out of the cell not sure what to do with himself, debating dream or reality. He stood opposite of officer Vin.

"You have this man's shadow. In a jar. In your pocket," Jacky said waving a hand in front of Vin's face, eyes open, but remained motionless. "Is he dead?"

"No. He's frozen in the ether."

"The what?"

"No time for that now. He'll be back to normal at first light. This experience will have been like a dream to him. The more he tries to remember, the more it will slip away and be forgotten."

"I'm not sure if I want to go anywhere with you, mister," Jacky said with a firm tone, although he still questioned his state of mind.

Silas took a deep breath. His eyes narrowed, brow furrowed. His stance solid and commanding.

"Your father sent me, Jacky," said Silas.

"You know my father?"

"No, I do not know your father. I owe the Rhino."

"The Rhino?! My dad's dad?"

"Yes. Your grandfather," said Silas.

"His knuckles were like baby rhino horns, as the story goes. I never knew him."

"Your father dream-spoke to me. There is a demon after you, Jacky. Your father called in on my debt to the Rhino. I am bound by honor and must bring you to safety. When was the last time you saw your father, Jacky?"

"I haven't seen him in years. He was caught transporting the red imp. Law man got him locked up somewhere I reckon.

"Ahh... red imp. Right, red absinthe is outlawed on the other side of the world, as well. Dangerous spirits."

"It's not my taste. It makes people crazy. My father was obsessed with it. He swore it showed him things."

"It's true. Your father is a Seer in the Dream. Red absinthe gets him there. Listen up, Jacky, your father is trapped in the red imp haze and he's running out of tomorrows."

"Do you know where he is?"

"I have an idea of his whereabouts."

"Take me to him."

"I will. But first, there's a bit of business which demands my attention."

Under night sky, the horse and cottage-wagon carried

Silas and Jacky on a winding road. No music, only the rhythm of exhausting steam and gallop. The road cut through a forest of oak, pine and maple trees. Night critters and insects sang the nocturnal song. The air humid but with a biting chill which assailed the lungs.
"Tell me, Jacky, how did you come to be confined in previous accommodations?"
"I make my living traveling from town to town, breaking jaws and bruising ribs," he said with a smile and wink. "I know, I know. Gypsy boxing is illegal, but it's damn good money. Made a name for myself, the last few years. I was on my way to a big fight farther down the bayou, had every intention on just passing through Tiger Island. Happened to run into a fancy dressed fella who recognized me. He offered to be my manager, take a cut of my winnings. I said, 'no sir. I'm doing fine on my own.' It was easy to see his disappointment. Later that night, I was boozing it up with the preacher man at the whore house. I can only assume something was slipped into my drink because the next morning I woke up in the jailhouse. Had the worst hangover in my life. Hell, I couldn't even remember who I was at first. A few days passed, no body said a word to me. Then, I get a visit from that fancy dressed fella. He very politely asked me to reconsider his offer. Again, I refused. Well, that just about pissed him off. 'You'll rot in this cell before you ever box again,' he threatened."
"How long were you locked up?" Asked Silas.
"Almost a month, I reckon." Jacky shifted his weight,

relaxing into the idea that he was actually free. "How do you hunt demons?"

"The mechanical horse and caravan serve as bait," said Silas. "Have to draw them out. It's not easy to distinguish a normal person from someone demon possessed."

"Really?" Jacky pondered the idea.

"Demons obsess over human inventions. This steam powered horse will drive a demon to salivation. Every gear and piston teasing an ecstasy of demonic infatuation."

"So, you're going to do an exorcism?" Jacky asked.

"No. Exorcisms are just a quick fix. In all actuality, exorcism is merely chasing a demon out of one person and eventually into another."

"I guess that makes sense. So, how do you deal with demonic possession?"

"I take the head. You can't kill a demon, but you can take it's head with a certain sword, put it in a bag and bury it in a certain cemetery."

"That is wild." Jacky shook his head in disbelief. "Well, what about the person possessed? Aren't they innocent?"

Silas stared at Jacky for a few moments, said nothing. They traveled the winding road up the hill and stopped just before the clearing.

Silas disappeared into the caravan, within moments he emerged with sword and scabbard. The blade rung like a bell when unsheathed.

"Whoah! I ain't never seen a sword like it," said Jacky.

"It was made across the ocean on the other side of the world. Specifically for demon decapitation. Forged in a volcano and quenched in the piss of a red headed virgin."

At the edge of the clearing, Silas and Jacky surveilled the premises. Gas lights burned bright throughout the house of Hieronymus.

"Stay here with the caravan. I will be back shortly." Jacky stood there with a blank stare. Before he could get a word out, Silas was gone.

Silas made a mad dash for the mansion. Although he moved incredibly fast, his footsteps made no noise. He slipped in through the back door. His movement swift and quiet thru the back of the house and against the dining room door which was slightly ajar. He peered through the opening. The angle blocked full view of the room, but he could see Hieronymus, a set of twins and most of another man. Judging by the voices, at least two more people there just beyond sight. Hieronymus and the other man were in conversation. The twins, a boy and girl no older than eight years old. The girl sat there quietly, the boy restless and fidgety.

"It's that fancy dressed fella... and the god damn preacher man!" said Jacky just under a whisper.

"What the bloody hell are you doing here?! I told you to wait in the caravan." Frustration saturated Silas's words.

Jacky crouched low, peeping through the opening, as well.

"Must have been that son-of-a-bitch... slipped

something in my drink that night at the whore house."
Silas pulled Jacky away from the door.
"Jacky, stop talking. Return to the caravan this instant!"
Silas demanded. "The only wager here is death."
"Well, I've never been to a demon fight before." Jacky
pulled away.
Both Silas and Jacky chanced another glance into the
dining room.
"Now wait. Hang on. You can't kill those kids," said
Jacky.
"They are not what you think. We have indeed
ventured into a nest of demons," said Silas.
Large covered platters were placed on the table in
front of each child. Removed covers revealed blissfully
sleeping human babies. The kind of deep sleep
induced by a good feeding from a warm fat tit. Each
demon child gently lifted the infants into the air. In
unison, both children unhinged their jaws and took the
babies' heads with one bite, tilting back with mouths
wide to drink the warm blood draining from fat babe
headless body dangling by ankles.
"I... can't. I'm going to..." stuttered Jacky. The
traumatizing sight gut punched Jacky to his soul.
Disbelief, shock and nausea assailed his physical
and mental faculties. His throat felt swollen like
the moment before vomit charges exit. It only took
a couple dry heaves to entice a liquid upheaval.
Involuntary reflex moved Silas away from Jacky's
spewing and through the door into the dining room.
The family stopped and stared with confused and

bewildered faces, Silas with drawn sword at mid guard and Jacky wiping puke from his chin.

The full room view revealed in the center of the table, a large metal cage which contained a freaked out Vesper. Her eyes met with Silas's. For a few heartbeats, the room seemed to be void of all sound.

"Get me the fuck out of here!" screamed Vesper.

Silas locked eyes with Hieronymus.

Hieronymus stood, slammed his fists on the table uttering something in demon tongue. The preacher man dove under the table for safety.

"That was a summon for lesser-demons," said Silas. "You'll need to pull yourself together rather quickly now, young Hammer."

The unmistakable sound of hooves charged on hardwood floors. As the hooves grew louder, Jacky's heart pounded harder and faster. The stomach purge addressed his nausea, felt his legs back under him. He never experienced such a kaleidoscope of emotions, but once he had a taste of this brand of adrenaline, he wanted more.

Jacky had his fists up, chin tucked scanning the room. Hooves echoed off the hardwood floors from every direction. Anticipation drove adrenaline to extreme levels. The floor rumbled behind. He knew it was something big and fast approaching but unprepared for what he turned to see. It looked like a man-sized baboon goat standing on hind legs. The creature's arms were man-like, covered in long coarse hair. Torso squamous and gaunt. A foul stench followed the lesser-demons into the room. Jacky stood there frozen, unable to react. His jaw dropped at the site as did his guard.

The lesser-demon roared as it launched attack on defenseless Jacky. Demon claws, inches away from ripping out Jacky's throat, suddenly changed direction with the flash of a blade, on intervened trajectory.

"Jacky! Snap out of it, man!" Silas shouted.

Silas moved with extraordinary speed and cut down the flailing one-handed abomination. Demon blood spewed covering Jacky. In a casual manner, Jacky wiped the blood from his mystified face in one motion. Silas stood opposite of the slack-jawed Jacky.

Desperation took desperate measure.

"You're going to get us both killed!" The open palm of Silas's hand connected with Jacky's cheek. The impact left a red hand-shaped imprint.

"Jacky Hammer!" Silas shouted.

Cognition chased away paralysis. Jacky returned to coherence.

"Fight!" Silas shouted.

Four more lesser-demons entered the room seemingly from nowhere.

Hieronymus's wife disappeared into the opposite room. The demon children leapt high into the air and clung to the ceiling, hissing at Jacky and Silas.

Jacky charged the nearest lesser-demon as it charged him and delivered an obnoxious dropkick which broke several of the lesser-demon's ribs. He didn't give the hell creature time to recover. Jacky's fists were swift and relentless. A right jab fractured it's sternum, the left jab broke it clean through. A right uppercut shattered the jawbone of the baboon headed beast. It dropped to the floor. The other lesser-demon on Jacky's side nearly had him, but he dodged diseased claws of the defiled.

Jacky circled around the lesser-demon effortlessly. Before the hell creature had time to turn around an oversized fist fractured lower spinal cord. The demon slumped writhing. A solid boot stomp shattered the rest of the spine. Jacky turned to assess Silas's situation. The blood spewing from the shoulders of a headless lesser-demon indicated Silas fared well. Jacky rushed towards Silas to help. Something slimy landed on Jacky's shoulder. It burned like hell fire. Another one landed on Jacky's back, the pain from the burning stopped him in his tracks. He desperately tried to wipe it away, but only spread it and caused his hands to burn. Jacky scanned the room. He ducked a third wad of slime. The demon kids on the ceiling were spitting on Jacky with their acid like saliva.

Jacky pulled a chair from the table and hurled it at the ceiling knocking one of the hybrid demonlings to the floor, rendering it unconscious. Jackie jumped onto the table which gave him plenty reach to land a solid blow to the second hybrid. Both fell to the floor, one unconscious, Jacky on his feet.

Silas reached into his leather thigh bag, retrieved a chain grenade and pulled the pin. He tossed it at the last lesser-demon. The high tension spring at the center unraveled itself with extreme potential, launching razor chains in every direction. Several chains pushed through the soft parts of the lesser-demon, the rest wrapped themselves around torso and limbs. The razor wire-like chains sliced with deep constriction into demon flesh on the verge of amputation. A standoff between Silas and Hieronymus gave them time to measure one another. The proverbial 'eye of the storm' moment when time stops for an instant, only for all hell to break loose again. Both sets of eyes glared with furious anger.

Silas noticed movement from behind him. He managed to sidestep a lethal stab wound, although the blade plunged deep into his left arm, ripping its way out. The wife swung the blade again, but only sliced through air, a mortal defining mistake which left her open for an easy kill. With one fluid motion, Silas removed the wife's head. It rolled under the table next to the preacher man. His scream sounded like it came from a prepubescent girl instead of a full grown man. Consciousness abandoned him as he pissed himself.

Silas felt blood running down the back of his arm. He knew he had to make short work of this last encounter or he would soon bleed out.

Silas, sword in high guard, charged Hieronymus. Jacky attacked Hieronymus from behind, attempting to trap the demon patriarch in a choke hold.

"No!" Silas cursed the distance and air between them.

"Get away from him, you fool!" Silas ordered.

Jacky did not comply until he began to lose grip. Hieronymus transformed into his true eldritch form. A demon-kind known to be of the baphomet bloodline, an elite demon blood.

Leathery wings grew out of Hieronymus's back, causing Jacky to lose more grip and leverage, his feet dangled high from the floor. Course hair covered the three eyed goat head. It gnashed its teeth into Jacky's right forearm removing a chunk of flesh. The Hieronymus-baphomet flung Jacky away from it's back and followed through with another attack meant for Jacky's mortal dispatch. Demon talons sliced into Jacky's abdomen, but not deep enough to spill guts. The baphomet howled in anguish, Silas's demon killing sword pierced spinal cord, pushing through the other side. With a turn of the wrist and slice, Silas disemboweled the Hieronymus-baphomet. Loops of intestine fell out. The hell beast dropped to the floor, unable to use it's huge horse-like legs. The Hieronymus-baphomet pushed itself up with its arms exposing it's goat head to vulnerability. Silas took it with one swift arcing chop. He immediately dropped the demon head into the bag. While yelling at Jacky, he released Vesper from her cage.

"Jacky... get up! We have to go... now!"

"Silas... I just need to sit here... for a few moments," said Jacky. His skin pallid and clammy. Blood pouring from his arm and trickling from stomach.

"No! We don't have time. This was the easy part. What lies ahead of us is much more difficult."

"What do you mean?" Jacky asked.

"There is a horde of very angry and vengeful demons

about to come looking for this," Silas held up the bag
containing Hieronymus's head.

"A horde of demons?" asked Jacky and Vesper
simultaneously, as if they rehearsed the line many
times.

"Yes. And hell hounds." Silas added. "The bag will
help kill the demon scent, but distance between us and
them is our best ally and chance for survival."

Silas and Vesper each took an arm, helped Jacky to his
feet.

They heard howls and shrieks in the distance. It did
not take them long to get back to Silas's mechanical
horse and cottage-wagon. Silas sat behind the steering
wheel, Jacky and Vesper on the passenger side, demon
head in the middle. Silas put on a peculiar pair of
goggles, pulled a few levers and released the brake. The
mechanical horse reared up on it's hind legs, billowed
steam from it's nostrils and charged forward.

"This is going to be one hell of a ride."

POLYESTER SUITS
AT THE
PINK FLAMINGO INN

"Oh shit! They found us, get back inside." Dew
couldn't believe it. He and Maggie were so careful
on their way to the Pink Flamingo Inn. The plan well
thought out for months. Positive no one had followed
them. They even switched cars on the way as an added
precaution. Maggie was halfway out of the door when
Dew spotted Hex's men. He knew exactly who they
were. Johnny Fingers and Bag Man, two of Hex's most
notorious goons. Dew closed the door as casually
as possible trying not to draw the goon's attention.
Maggie began to hyperventilate.
"Oh my god oh my god oh my god. What are we
going to do?!" Overwhelming fear trembled her voice.
She was freaking out. Tears rolled down her rosey
cheeks.

"Calm down, baby. Calm down," Dew spoke in a surprisingly composed tone. "Just take a few deep breaths with me, sweetheart." The two of them breathed deeply in unison for a few moments. Dew noticed how particularly gorgeous her eyes were behind the streaming tears. The color of her beautiful irises were accented by a frame of irritated redness. She was the most beautiful girl he had ever seen. He often proclaimed to be the luckiest guy in the world to have landed such an extraordinary looking girlfriend. She had the movie star model quality about her. Maggie rarely wore make-up, she didn't need it. Dew lost count of how many times random strangers, men and women both, were innocently compelled to respectfully comment on her beauty. Maggie never completely comfortable with the compliments, but it sure made Dew proud.

"Ok. I'm ok now," hysterics subsided. Maggie wiped the tears away with the palms of her hands.

Dew had a way with people. His special talent persuasion. He could talk anybody into anything. The frequency of his voice resonated with people and his apple pie demeanor invited instant trust. Ever the clever man, he knew there was no chance to talk his way out of this dire situation. They would have to fight for thier lives.

"Look, there's only two of them and four of us. We can handle it," Dew reassured Maggie as she reluctantly forced a smile. The urge to kiss her was irresistable. Their lips locked for a momentary eternity of passion. Salty tears flavored her mouth.

The adjoined room was occupied by another couple, Hunter and Becky. They were all in it together. Hunter and Dew were lifelong friends. Hunter had never been accused of being the smartest fellow in any room, but loyalty undoubted. He would follow Dew to hell and back if Dew so much as asked. Becky made it a packaged deal. She was never far away from Hunter, they were almost joined at the hip. Becky, a bit more bright than Hunter, had him wrapped around her finger. Their love for each other paralleled Dew and Maggie's.

Dew crept up to the door. Just as he put his eye to the peep hole, he got a fish eye view of Johnny Fingers and Bag Man. The door knob turned slightly. It was locked, except for the top latch. Dew carefully moved it into lock position.

He silently mouthed the words, "Go to the back."

Maggie nodded her head.

There was a heavy slam against the door. The angel of disparity descended upon them. They quietly walked to the back of the room and pulled the heavy curtain back just enough to peep out the window. It was a very nice view of the Pink Flamingo Inn's swimming pool. To their horrified dismay, two more of Hex's hatchet men were on the opposite side of the pool. Dew hadn't seen either of these guys before, but they were dressed for shady business. Beware of polyester suits and exposed overly hairy chests adorned with gold neck chains.

"Tacky son-of-a-bitches always wearing high-waters," Dew whispered to Maggie. She stifled a giggle. "Hunter has the guns in his room." Dew hated guns. His experience with firearms amounted to beebee guns one summer at his grandparents house. On accident, he shot himself in the foot and never touched such a weapon with any amount of firepower again. Dew wanted Hunter to keep the firearms with him just in case things went south and indeed the plan had gone awry.

The fright in her eyes matched his. Dew tried to maintain a strong countenance, but he was noticeably out of his element. They were in too deep. Quietly, Dew and Maggie opened the door that joined the two rooms.

"Hunter has the guns," Dew thought to himself. Ever the clever man, he was putting together a plan of action. "We'll ambush them. We'll wait for them to walk through the door and we'll..."

As Maggie and Dew stepped into the next room, a wave of terror washed over them. Hunter and Becky were motionless on the floor with plastic bags over their heads. Bag Man already dispatched them. Maggie almost had time to scream, but Bag Man had prepared a moment sooner. A similar bag to Hunter and Becky's slipped over her head. It happened so fast. Too fast for Dew to process or react. He heard the familiar sound of a high pitched gunshot muffled by a silencer and then another almost immediately afterwards. Familiar not by first hand experience, but from gangster movies he

loved to watch. Those were his absolute favorites.
'As long as I can remember, I always wanted to be a gangster,' popped into his mind. A line from one of those movies he so obsessed with.

'You want to be a gangster, but you don't like guns? What kind of shit is that?' Hunter often harrassed Dew.

Dew felt a hammer blow to his gut and then to his chest. Something searing hot passed through his body and his body in succession met the floor, his eyes wide open in shock.

"They must have shot me. I'll just lay here. Pretend to be dead. Then I'll make a run for it when I get a chance. I just have to wait for the right opportunity."

He heard the commotion going on, but couldn't see what was happening. They were just beyond the range of his periphery. Maggie was being murdered a few feet away from him and there was nothing he could do about it.

"Hang on, Maggie, just hang on. Where did Hunter put the guns?" If only he knew, he would sneak to the guns, one in each hand and blast those high-water polyester wearing bastards to hell. Save Maggie's life in the nick of time, just like the movies.

The commotion stopped. A heavy thud heard and felt on the floor. Maggie was gone. Dew's heart shattered into a million shards of hurt. She was the only woman to have ever loved him. Guilt hammered nails made of pure heartache and reget. It was his fault she was dead.

Johnny Fingers entered the periphery. Dew dared not blink or move a muscle.

"Just play dead. Play possum until the time is right. Then I'll make my move. I'll get those bastards for Maggie."

Johnny Fingers reached into his pocket and pulled out a pair of gardening pruners with green rubber handles. He knelt down, tilted his head sideways almost parallel to Dew's.

"Don't blink. Don't move a muscle," Dew thought.

Johnny Fingers poked Dew in the eye with his stubby index finger, but no reaction or involuntary reflex. Dew amazed to have that much bodily control. "I must be in shock." Ordinary people perform superhuman feats during life or death situations and this was without a doubt one of those situations.

Johnny Fingers had a firm grip on Dew's right hand and raised it into full view. The green rubber handled gardening pruners were placed at the base of Dew's right pinky.

"Oh, this is going to suck," Dew prepared himself for what was surely coming next.

Snip. Dew's right hand fell to the floor minus a pinky. "I'm most definitely in shock," Dew assessed. "I didn't feel that at all."

Johnny Fingers's face back in full view stared directly into Dew's eyes. Johnny Fingers placed Dew's pinky in a plastic zip lock bag and then into his pocket. Out of the same pocket came a white handkerchief which he used to wipe the blood from the green handled gardening pruners.

"Shock must also affect the perception of time," Dew

contemplated.

Johnny Fingers was moving in slow motion. The same index finger that moments ago poked him in the eye was slowly creeping its way back to it once again, plus a thumb. Johnny Fingers used them to pull down Dew's eyelids. Closing the shades to the windows of his soul.

"Wait... wait... something's not right," Dew had a sudden sickening realization, "I'm dead."

THE GOLDEN BAND

Caleb looked at her, he couldn't believe she was leaving him. "We've been together for so long and been through so much," an attempt to convince her not to go. But, she remained motionless and without expression. She had not heard one word he said.

Speechless, his mind drifted back to the night they first met. A couple of his buddies, Terry and Nick, set up a blind date, but a reluctant Caleb feared the experience would be abysmal. As usual, his buddies convinced him to go.

Caleb, Terry and Nick arrived at the carnival as planned, but the 'total babes' were not there.

"I knew it," said Caleb. "I knew they wouldn't show up."

"Chill, Caleb. They'll be here. Females are always

fashionably late."

"Hey, Terry, Nick!" exclaimed a female voice from behind Caleb.

"Here comes our love goddesses now," Terry said.

"Yep," added Nick.

Caleb thought to himself, "here we go." He turned around expecting to see two asparagus looking hags, but instead, found two of the most gorgeous girls he had ever seen in his life. His mouth opened and his brow curled up in bewildered amazement.

"Pick up your jaw, son" Terry said with arrogance.

"Yeah, you're drooling on my shoes," Nick added.

"Ashley, Jade, this is Caleb," introduced Nick.

Caleb noticed Terry smile from ear to ear as he hugged Ashley.

Terry asked, "Where is Melody?"

"She's at the concessions. I'll go get her," Ashley replied. She turned, but before she left, looked Caleb up and down.

Caleb actually thought they were 'total babes'. Ashley was a goddess to him. Unfortunately, Melody was to be his date for the night.

"She's probably pretty hot," Caleb contemplated on what Melody would look like. "Look at her friends," convincing himself.

He watched Ashley as she walked to the concessions. She approached a girl with blonde hair, wearing shorts that were too short to be legal.

"She's got that California girl thing going on," he thought to himself, getting excited.

Caleb turned his back to her direction. As Ashley and Melody walked up, Caleb spun around giving his best 'James Dean'. When he saw Melody, he spun right back around and gasped, "Oh, God!"

Jade whispered, "She's got a great personality."

"Oh, God," Caleb let out again, as if it were vomit.

"Caleb, this is Melody," Ashley introduced.

Caleb quickly regained his composure. Being a well mannered guy, he figured politeness would be the best resolve to survive the night. He turned to see his date with cotton candy in one hand, buttered popcorn oozing down the other and a candied apple planted in her mouth. She wasn't the blonde beauty from California at all. She had the body, but her face looked like the wrong end of a dog.

"Hey, how ya doing, I'm Caleb. Nice to meet you."

"Hmm, Mmm, phmmph," Melody mumbled while the candied apple still in her mouth. She had no manners. Melody examined Caleb then Terry, with an analytical, greasy face. At the same moment, Terry was staring at Ashley as she stared at Caleb. Caleb was just trying not to look at anyone.

Melody pried the apple loose, "I want this one!" She then slapped a death grip around Terry's wrist with her sticky fingers. "Come on!" she ordered, nearly pulling Terry off his feet.

He was in total shock, "B... but"

Caleb noticed how much Melody and Terry strangely reminded him of a little girl dragging around a beat up

baby doll.
"Well, I guess it's me and you," Caleb said to Ashley. "I guess so," she replied, with a huge smile.
The group lost Melody and Terry in the crowd. Hours passed and the night was coming to an end. They decided to wait at their vehicles for Terry and Melody to show up. As they neared Ashley's car, a ruckus emanated from inside.
"Come on, stop. I don't do this on the first date." It wasn't a female voice that was heard. Oddly enough, it was Terry's.
"What are you kids doing?" Caleb asked in a teasing voice.
"Help!" cried Terry. His head popped up from the backseat.
Laughter erupted from the small group.
He broke himself free from Melody's iron clutches. His shirt was torn in the process and he had some sort of yellowish dribble from his lips down to the right side of his neck.
"Man, what do you have all over you?" asked Nick.
Ashley sniffed the air, "smells like... popcorn butter."
Jade giggled.
An embarrasssed and frustrated Terry shouted, "I'm outta here! Meet me at the Jeep." With the last bit of dignity he had left, Terry stormed off with half his shirt on and the other half flowing behind like a cape.
Caleb called out to him, "and put your clothes back on."
Laughter erupted again.

Melody stepped out from the backseat. She had the same familiar yellow dribble on her face except, a popcorn kernel was slowly sliding down her chin. Ashley and Caleb exchanged phone numbers and said good night with a simple, warm hug. Their relationship blossomed into a rare magical kind only read in stories or seen in movies.

"Please, baby, don't let it end like this." Caleb tried reasoning with Ashley, but she didn't hear his plee.

"You can't leave me, you're still wearing my ring." Caleb looked at the shining band of gold still on her left hand. It was too big for her so she stuffed a small piece of cloth between the ring and her finger for a snug fit. It was Caleb's senior ring. He wore hers on a chain around his neck. They exchanged these rings a few months into the relationship with the promise to stay together forever.

They were together for three years. Ashley and Caleb were never a part. "Two peas in a pod," their parents would say. Rarely seen one without the other. If you did, it seemed like eating cereal with a fork. It just wasn't right.

Arguments peppered the third year of their relationship. They fought about three simple words. Caleb never told Ashley that he loved her. She told him all the time, but his reply would be, "me, too." Although Ashley knew Caleb loved her deeply, she grew annoyed to hear "me, too" instead of "I love you."

That problem became one major regret.

"God, Ashley, please don't leave me. You mean

everything to me. Remember our promise? We promised on these rings." He held her hand and showed her the ring around his neck that meant so much to him, but she remained cold and emotionless. He kissed her hand. A tear fell from his cheek. "You know what I'm saying. I know I never told you before, but... you know I do." Another tear fell from his cheek to hers, "I love you." In hysterics Caleb shouted, "I love you! I love you!" He felt a firm hand on his shoulder. It was Terry's.

"Come on, man. It's over. Let's go," Terry said with broken words.

After a minute or so, Caleb said calmly, "No, I can't leave her." He bent over her casket, kissed her lips, and whispered, "I love you." Caleb stood and said, "I can't leave her."

About the Author

Boon Businelli is a musician, wordsmith and professional tattooist in the pop culture convention circuit

"My passion is creating works of art that provide a moment of escape from Real Life. Until this book, most people knew me as a musician and professional tattoo artist. In my late teens, I formed a band to this day retains a cult following. This band opened the door to my almost twenty year career of professional tattooing. Tattooing enabled me to jump on the pop culture convention circuit in 2012. The only degree I have is from the School of Hard Knocks. I wrote the first five of these stories at the beginning of 2018. The last story, The Golden Band, I wrote sometime in the mid 90's. It is actually the first short story I had ever written and included it for sentimental reasons. I strive to become a better version of myself everyday; to become a better artist, wordsmith and multi-dimensional being of infinite energy."

- Boon

Acknowledgements

I dedicate this book to myself, I couldn't have done it without me.

Thanks to my beta readers:

Chip Lechner
Denise Hollis Romero
Ethan Tyrell
Abigail Hammond
Endsville - Saint of the Hive
Stephanie Eli

To become a beta reader, contact
pikeycamp@gmail.com

To become part of the cyberspace community, go to
Shadow in a Jar @pikeycamp